GRUMPY PANTS

words & pictures by
CLAIRE MESSER

SCHOLASTIC INC.

Penguin was in a bad mood.
A very bad mood.

He didn’t know why
and he didn’t care.

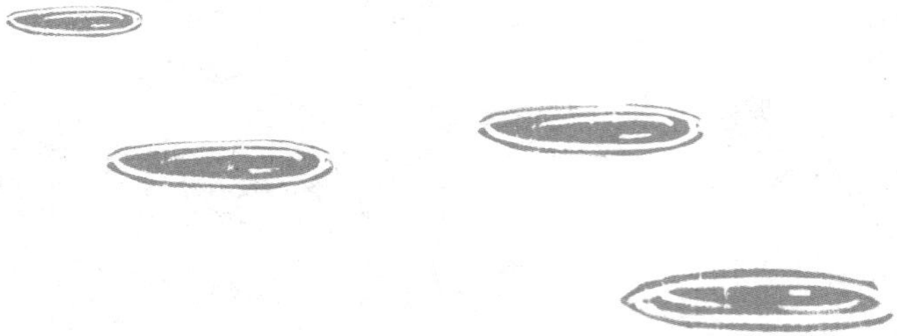

He stomped his feet
all the way home.

He pulled off his grumpy coat
and kicked off his grumpy boots.

But he was still grumpy.

He tried to shake it off.

But he was still grumpy.

So he pulled off one grumpy sock
and then the other.

But he was still grumpy.

So he took off his grumpy overalls...

Nope. Still grumpy.

Finally, he took off his
grumpy underpants.

“I’m still grumpy, you know.”

Then penguin took a deep breath
and he counted...

One...

two...

three...

SPL

ASH!

The water was nice and cold.
Penguin played with his duck.

He hid under the water and made
himself a bubble beard.

Little by little, he was starting
to feel much better.

It was time to get out of the tub.

He put on his favorite pajamas.

And he had a steaming
cup of hot chocolate.

He read his favorite book.

He found his favorite teddy
and climbed into bed.

As Penguin fell asleep, he knew that tomorrow would be a good day

because all the grumpiness
had been washed away.

For my big sister, Kirsten, and my husband, Simon, thanks for teaching me all about hissy fits.

ISBN 978-1-338-25339-9

12 11 10 9 8 7 6 5 4 3 2 17 18 19 20 21 22

Printed in the U.S.A. 40

First Scholastic printing, October 2017

Design by Jordan Kost